A CHRISTMAS NANNY FOR THE COWBOY

KRINGLE CHRISTMAS TREE RANCH

MIA BRODY

This is a work of fiction. Names, characters, places, and incidents either are the product of the author's imagination or are used fictitiously. Any resemblance to actual persons, living or dead, events, or locales is entirely coincidental.

Copyright © 2022 by Mia Brody

All rights reserved. No part of this book may be reproduced or used in any manner without written permission of the author except for the use of quotations in a book review.

1
MICAH

"Five minutes. We'll just be in here five minutes," I promise the little girl in my arms. I never expected to wake up with a baby girl on my doorstep. But that's what happened two days ago. The only clue was a note left with her. *She's yours. Take good care of her, Micah.*

Except she's not mine. That isn't denial talking. It's cold, hard science. Despite my nearly thirty years of age, I've never been with anyone. I've poured everything into making the Kringle Christmas Tree Ranch more profitable. No one has ever caught my eye. Well, not until the little thing who works here at Emma May's grocery store did a few weeks ago. But I'm too old and too gruff for a sweet woman like Chloe.

Abby blinks up at me. Actually, I think she's squinting. I'm not sure how well babies can see. I add it to the list of things I'll be searching on my phone later. As it was, it took me all of yesterday to choose a name. There wasn't anything to identify her in the car seat or diaper bag. Just two bottles of formula and that damn note.

A smarter man would have called the sheriff. But Sheriff Luke is obligated to tell child protective services. Next thing you know she's being bounced around from home to home.

I was just like her once. I was a foster kid who kept getting thrown away for one reason or another. No matter how good I tried to be or how hard I worked, I couldn't make anyone want me. I won't let that happen to her. I won't let it be her story.

I called in Cash, the town doctor, to examine her as soon as I found her. He estimates she's only about two weeks old. He didn't ask me too many questions. I'm considered an upstanding member of the community. Which means as long as there are no blood tests and everyone takes my word for it, this will be fine.

"So, the thing is, grocery stores are loud sometimes, and I can't really help that," I tell her. It's my job to introduce her to the world. That's what the parenting podcast I've been listening to in between her naps tells me.

If I'd had any other option, I would have left her at the house. But my brothers are struggling to keep the ranch running in my absence, and the foster parents I met when I had just turned eighteen are sick with a cold. Even if they weren't, they're busy with lives of their own. They don't need to be raising a kid again, which means I need someone to help me out.

There's a thread on the Courage County social board where townsfolk can ask Santa for something. People can post anonymously or as themselves. I posted asking for a nanny for Christmas. Figured it was probably better than asking for a date with the dark-haired cashier who features in my dreams.

Abby grunts and starts rooting around my chest. I manage to juggle a bottle of formula out of the truck and get it into her mouth before she can start screaming her head off.

She's beautiful and amazing and also the loudest thing I've ever heard. She eats constantly, about every two hours. Cash said it was normal and even dropped off some formula to get me through these first two days with her. It's only been forty-eight hours, and I don't know how new parents do this.

She's so tiny and she needs constant care. My every thought is now about her and whether she's happy.

"See? That's better now, isn't it?" I croon as I wander into Emma May's grocery store like this is normal. Like I'm always around town with a baby tucked in my arms. I chose the early morning hours to minimize the amount of people she would be exposed to. I won't hide her. Not ever. I'm damn proud of this little girl. But the world has to be a scary place when you're that small and surrounded by strangers.

Warm air greets us inside the store, a welcome relief from the cold winter. It's not long now until Christmas. I wonder what babies want for the holidays. I wonder if she's even noticed the tree in my living room. Can she identify objects yet?

I glance around the brightly lit, clean store. I scan the register area and tell myself that I'm not disappointed when it's empty. I wasn't looking for a certain brunette with the shy smile and sweet curves. Nope, wasn't looking for Chloe at all.

Since the store is mostly empty, I thread my way back to the baby care section while keeping one eye on the bottle. Cash had rules about stopping to burp her through the feedings. Said something about air getting trapped in her little tummy. *Fuck, there's a lot to remember with a baby.*

Still, I figured out how to run the ranch. It was making some money but not a lot when I took over as manager at barely eighteen. I'm pretty sure the only reason that Mr. Kringle gave me the job was because I'd tried to do everything else at the farm. I hadn't been very good at any of it. He must have finally figured that at least my brain might be useful.

I've done him proud in the time since. I consistently double the ranch's profits and ever since then, he leaves me alone to do whatever I want. In fact, he won't make a decision about the ranch without consulting me.

I'm so lost in thought that I don't even hear Emma May approach as I glance at the rows of baby formula. Each one promises to be gentle on her tummy while being fortified with vitamins needed for her growth.

"And who is this little one?" Emma May's silver hair is in its usual long braid down her back, and she peers over her bifocals. She's a tiny little thing that barely comes up to my chest, so I crouch lower, letting her see my Abby.

"Such a pretty girl," she admires and accepts my

daughter when I pass the little bundle to her. She's had five children of her own and fostered countless others. That's the thing about a place like Courage County. Your past doesn't matter. Everyone is welcome here. "You didn't tell me you have a daughter."

I haven't introduced her to anyone but family yet. Even then, my parents only got to see her on video call since they've been sick. "I didn't know until just recently."

Truth is, I'm a little worried about Abby's mama. You don't leave a baby on a doorstep because you think you've got a lot of options. Given how she's only around two weeks old, her mom could be in need of medical care too. I wish I had some clue as to her identity, some way to reach out and let her know that I can help. That I'll keep Abby safe and warm and make sure she grows up with all the love in the world.

Emma May clucks her tongue. "Well, where's her mama?"

Sweat trickles down my back. Whatever I say in this moment will be repeated across town for years. Little Abby will most likely hear it when she's old enough, so I settle on the best thing I know to say, "She's not in her life at the moment. But I'm hopeful one day things will be different."

Without missing a beat, she pops the bottle from Abby's mouth and keeps her entertained long enough to burp her. How she did that without Abby letting out one of her screams, I'll never know. "Let's hope so. Christmas is a time for miracles."

I glance over at the baby in her arms. "It sure is."

After I'm done getting everything on Cash's list and a few things that Emma May insisted he must have forgotten, Abby is sleeping again. All this kid does is sleep and eat. The parenting blogs tell me this is normal, and she'll eventually become a little more alert. But it scared the shit out of me at first.

As I approach the registers, I notice Chloe is here now. My mouth goes dry, and my heart starts pounding. I've never talked with her other than to exchange pleasantries. Sure, I think she's damn beautiful, and I'd love nothing more than to take her up against the side of my truck with her fingernails digging into my arms and her sweet voice screaming my name. But I'm too old for her. I won't be the creepy guy who leers at her while she works, so mainly I keep my mouth shut around her.

"Did you get stuck on babysitting duty this morning?" Chloe asks as she scans the extra-large pack of diapers. Forget selling Christmas trees. The ranch is going to sell diapers. We'll make a fortune within a week.

"She's mine." It's stupid to be so nervous about this. It's not like the curvy woman in front of me is anyone to me. At this rate, she never will be.

The only hint that this news has affected her is the slight pause before she reaches for the next item. "I didn't realize you were a father."

I pretend to survey the offerings of gum and try to ignore the expression on her face. Why does she look disappointed? Nah, I'm imagining that. This is the problem with being nearly thirty and never having taken the time to date. I don't know how to read a woman. "It's new."

Now she's scanning without looking up at me, letting her dark hair fall like a curtain. My fingers itch to smooth it back so I can see her facial expression again. "What's her name?"

"Abigail. Abigail Kringle," I answer. Technically, I'm not a Kringle. They never adopted me the way they did my sister. I was already eighteen by the time I met them. But everyone calls me a Kringle, and with the baby and all, I figure I should embrace that. Give my little girl a last name she can be proud of.

She finally looks up then and says softly, "That's a real pretty name."

Yeah, I've read this whole thing wrong. She's not into me at all. I'm not disappointed, not even a little bit. I take my bagged groceries, ignoring the jolt that goes down my arm when our fingertips brush. "Well, I asked Santa for a nanny this year. Maybe the big, jolly guy will do me a solid."

I guess it's a good thing I didn't ask Santa for a date with the pretty cashier. I'd have made a fool of myself in front of the whole town.

2
CHLOE

He has a baby. I really am dumb.

All these weeks of watching him come to the store and hoping he'd ask me out, I've been a fool. I never seen him with a girlfriend, and the gossip around town is that all three of the fine-looking Kringle brothers are single. Well, except for West. He's officially off the market since he's dating Cassie.

But clearly, Micah was seeing someone secretly. He takes trips out of town regularly, something about business for the Christmas tree ranch he runs with his family. He must have a girlfriend who doesn't live in Courage County. I can't help but wonder what she looks like. What kind of woman catches a gruff cowboy like Micah's attention?

As soon as he leaves, Emma May hurries up to me. "Thanks for opening the store today."

She's wearing a sheepish look, and I know she feels bad. She had to let me go due to financial problems three days ago. But when she needed someone to open up this morning, I volunteered without hesitating. It's just the way people are in Courage County. You help a friend, no matter what.

"I'm glad I could help," I answer, feeling my stomach churn from my encounter with Micah. I wish I'd known about the baby sooner. I wouldn't have wasted all this time thinking about him and waiting for him.

She wrings her hands. "Any luck?"

"Not so far, but I'm sure something will turn up." Normally, Ernie and Lorna at the diner are always looking for an extra set of hands but they were full up. Austin from the flower shop doesn't need help either. Today, I'll go see Mallory at Sew Cute. Maybe she has a job for me.

Three days later, I have to admit defeat. There's no one in town who will hire me. I'm still good on rent for the next month. But it's the Christmas season, and I know my mama could use help. I left our tiny town in Georgia that had no opportunities to find full-time work. I send money back home every week to help with my siblings. But if this keeps up, I won't have anything to give her, and my heart hurts at the idea of my brothers and sisters going without.

Every morning, I scan the local newspaper and the social media group for the town. No one is hiring…except Micah and his silly request to Santa for a nanny. Technically, I could do the job. I mean, I'm the oldest of eight kids. I've definitely changed some diapers and handed out some bottles. It's not the job that has me hesitating. It's the idea of working closely around Micah. I'd see him every day, think about him every day. *Like you're not already doing that.*

But the phone call from my mama finally forces my hand. Wendy is sick again and she needs an antibiotic. Everything is expensive but when you have no health insurance and a limited income, you have to choose between paying the doctor and buying needed medication. Mama managed the doctor fees, but the prescription is on me.

I borrow against my rent money with my gut churning. Meanwhile, I'm on the phone to Mama and reassuring her it's fine. "I had a little in savings. You just help Wendy and don't worry about it."

After the online transfer is done, I see Micah's post again. Screw it. I'll find a way to be around him and stay professional. My siblings are counting on me, and I won't disappoint them.

Before I can talk myself out of it, I hitch a ride from Walker to the Kringle Ranch. He used to be the grumpiest cowboy then he fell in love with Jenna from the Feed & Seed store. The way he looks at her, you'd think she's responsible for making sure the sun rises every morning. I want a man to look at me that way one day. I wish that man could be Micah but that won't ever happen now.

When I arrive at the ranch, part of me regrets not calling ahead, but I was afraid I would lose my nerve and never show up. The farm is huge and sprawling. There's an old barn, a gift shop, and a long train decorated like a locomotive delivering toys. To the south of that is a home. Beyond the home, miles and miles of forest. A closer look has me realizing it's the area where the trees are grown.

"This may have been a bad idea," I mutter under my breath as I survey the buildings, trying to decide which one Micah might be in. I don't even know where to go first.

"That's how all my best stories start," a deep voice says.

I turn to see Ledger Kringle. He's always hanging out with Peyton, the bartender from Liquid Courage. He pulls off his cream-colored Stetson and gives me an apologetic glance. "Sorry, I didn't mean to scare you. What can I do for you?"

"I'm looking for Micah. About the nanny position."

He looks me up and down, a grin spreading over his face. "I'll take you to him."

I walk beside him as we take a winding path toward a big building.

"How long has the Kringle Ranch been in your family?" I ask Ledger as I try to keep up with him. He's so long-legged that it's hard for me.

He notices and slows his stride. "I don't reckon I know. A few generations, I suppose. The Kringles adopted me when I was about fifteen. Just like they did Micah and Cassie."

Weird, I didn't know they weren't all siblings. They always act like it every time I see them together. They're always bickering and teasing each other and laughing. It makes me miss my family.

Leaving our little town in Georgia was one of the hardest things I've ever done. There wasn't enough money for all of us to go. So, Mama scraped together enough cash to buy me a bus ticket.

I've been on my own ever since, bouncing from town to town. Courage County is the place I've stayed at the longest but if Micah doesn't hire me, I might have to find somewhere new. The thought of leaving this warm community makes my heart hurt. It has nothing to do with a certain gruff cowboy.

Ledger stops in front of a brick building that's small but neatly kept with window boxes out front. There are even seasonal plants in them. He knocks once on the red door before he's pushing inside and gesturing for me to follow.

"Hey, Micah," he calls. "Found a pretty little thing on the path here."

Micah looks up from his desk. It's cluttered with paperwork all around him. He's got Abby in one arm while cradling a phone between his shoulder and his head. The dark circles under his eyes tell me that he hasn't been sleeping well. I guess that shouldn't be a surprise given that he's just become a new father. But the sight makes me want to go to him. I want to brush the dark hair from his eyes and reassure him that he's not alone anymore.

With a muttered curse, he ends the phone call and glares at his brother. "What the duck is she doing here?"

Ledger shrugs but the entire time, he looks like

the cat who ate the canary. "I don't know. I was too distracted by how pretty she is to ask her. Maybe you should."

Something dark and possessive crosses Micah's features. "Out. Now."

I take two quick steps backward, prepared to flee his wrath. "No, not you. You stay. Ledge is leaving."

Ledger tips his head toward me, amusement still on his face. "Seems my work is done. Good luck with grumpy pants here."

Micah growls. He actually growls at Ledger.

But his brother just laughs as he takes three long strides to the door. "See you soon."

The moment we're alone, Micah's scowl only deepens. "Ignore Ledger. He's...well, he's Ledger."

"He seems nice enough," I offer.

There's another growl. I'm beginning to think he's not a cowboy at all. He's a caveman—a big, grumpy caveman. "What can I do for you?"

I twist the bottom of my shirt. Now that I'm here, I'm suddenly nervous. If he tells me he doesn't want me for this job, it'll be worse than being rejected by Austin or Mallory. They might not have given me a job, but I don't lie awake at night thinking about them.

But Micah is a different story. Sometimes, when

I'm alone in my bed and I remember the way he looks when he's scowling, my fingers drift into my panties. I caress my swollen folds and imagine it's him doing it.

I imagine that he's whispering into my ear, calling me his dirty girl, and telling me how slick I am. Would he nip at my skin? Put his blunt finger deep into my weeping channel? Would he make me come just from touching my pussy and murmuring filthy things into my ear?

Abby starts screeching, and her loud sounds pull me from my fantasies. The fantasies that are never going to come true anyway.

"The job. I'm here for the job," I answer the question he asked while tuning out the baby's noise. Growing up with so many siblings has taught me how to handle noise coming from multiple directions and still stay on task.

He looks me up and down while trying unsuccessfully to calm his daughter. "You ever operated a chainsaw?"

"I didn't think it would be necessary." What is the man expecting me to do, build a cradle from a tree that I've cut down on his property? Seems like a hell of an employment test.

"Operating a chainsaw is useful when cutting

firewood," he answers, his tone barely hiding his annoyance. He's so different than when he's at the store. I'm not sure if it's me or Abby's crying that's got him on edge. Maybe it's a bit of both.

"And that's part of the job?" At this point, I'm pretty desperate for employment. Even if being a nanny for Micah has some unusual tasks, I don't care. I just want money to take care of my family.

"Yep, right there in the description. Door is behind you. Have a nice day." He turns his attention back to the screaming baby girl that he's still trying in vain to comfort.

I can't believe this. He's being so thickheaded. I'm right here and I'm willing to help with Abby. "It really seems you can't afford to be picky about who you hire right now. Maybe try swaddling her."

He frowns at me. "Swaddling."

I gesture for him to pass me the crying child. He hesitates until her volume grows then he finally relinquishes her to me. I drop to my knees on the rug and settle her on top of the blanket before quickly swaddling her. She's quiet within seconds, her eyes already starting to drift closed.

"How did you know to do that?" His voice rumbles in my ear. I didn't even hear him come around the desk or realize he was leaning over us.

For some crazy reason, I like the feeling. I like the idea that he's over both of us, protecting me and Abby from the scary world.

"Secrets of being a nanny," I answer with a wink. I hope he can't hear how loud my heart is racing.

"The job." His cheeks flush slightly beneath his beard. "You were looking for the nanny job, not the one I posted this morning. Sorry. Sleep deprived dad here."

"I thought stacking firewood would be an unusual task." I continue holding Abby because he hasn't asked for her back. "Swaddling is thought to remind babies of life in the womb. It probably comforts her to feel close to her mother."

Sadness flickers across his face. "She isn't around."

I lean out and put a hand on his arm, feeling his strong muscles tense underneath my touch. "I'm sorry, Micah. That must be hard on you."

There are a million questions I want to ask him about her. Were they close? Are they still in touch? Was it a one-night thing or a long relationship? Why aren't they together anymore? But it doesn't seem like the place or time to ask anything.

He nods to his sleeping daughter. "Consider yourself hired. And maybe forget about the mix-up."

I can't help the smile. This job is exactly what I needed. The fact that my boss is the best-looking cowboy in all of Courage County has nothing to do with my excitement. Not even a little bit.

"How soon can you move in?"

3
MICAH

All right, so it wasn't supposed to be a live-in position. But I'm a greedy bastard. I'll say and do whatever it takes to get Chloe living under my roof. If that makes me a monster, I can live with that.

I just need to know she's safe. She's been losing weight; those precious curves are fading. I thought I noticed it in the grocery store, but I couldn't be sure. Now I'm absolutely positive. She's losing weight and she looks tired. Even a little discouraged.

When she first came in here, asking about the job, I could barely see past the blinding rage I felt toward Ledger. Call me an asshole but I don't want any man around Chloe. I want to be the only one she sees, and when she looked at him, it felt like I'd been punched in the gut.

"Move in?" She sputters the words.

"It's a full-time position," I answer as if I haven't been making this whole thing up on the spot. Her hair looks so soft. Would it be weird if I leaned close to sniff an employee's hair? Probably. Definitely.

She's barely been hired two minutes and I'm already in danger of losing my fucking mind. This is not going well.

When Abby lets out a contented sigh in her arms, Chloe's expression softens. I want to lean over and give my kid a high five. She may not realize it, but she just sealed the deal for me.

"For how long?"

"A year," I say because telling her forever is probably a bad idea.

"I would save on rent." Dammit, is that why she's losing weight and looking so tired, because she's under financial pressure?

The thought makes me sick. I don't want Chloe to be worried about anything. It's time to sell her on this. "My spare bedroom has a private bathroom with its own shower and tub."

Fuck, now I'm thinking about Chloe naked and that's not good. I need to be thinking professional thoughts. Nanny thoughts. "Plus, you'd be close to

Abby. Not that I expect you to watch her every night."

"Maybe we could trade off nights."

"Sure," I answer, already knowing that even if I have the night off, I won't take it. My brain is different these days. Everything is about Abby and if she so much as sniffles at night, I'm awake. I used to be able to sleep through a hurricane. Now she makes the tiniest squeak and I'm fully alert.

She beams at me, a relieved smile on her face. "I can move in tomorrow, if that's good."

"How's Abby?" Ledger asks as I shove a big bite of burger into my mouth. West brought the ones from Ernie's that I like so much. Now the three of us are eating lunch together in my office. We have to go out later and work on one of the tractors. It's the worst time of year for our machinery to break down, which means it always does.

"Fussy." Cash said it's normal for her to go through periods where she seems fussier. He called it growing pains. But I hate it, makes me feel like I'm failing at this parenting thing. What would Abby's mom say if she could see her now? Would she be happy with the job I'm doing, or would she regret giving her to me and take her back?

My heart seizes at the thought. I can't let her go. She's the reason my heart beats now. Well, her and a certain brunette. Which is why I spend as little time with Chloe as possible. I don't want her figuring it out and feeling uncomfortable around me.

"Babies are like that, according to Mom," West says. Ever since he got together with my sister, he talks a lot about families and babies and marriage.

I grunt in response. They're on the other side of the desk, getting crumbs and special sauce on my paperwork. With Chloe here, I should be catching up on some of it. But I'm not. Seems I spend a little too much time thinking about those kissable lips to get much done.

Mom has been pestering me to hire someone to help me in the office. She said something or another about how I work too much or too hard. I'm not entirely sure. I'd started thinking about Chloe again and there went any hope I had of concentrating.

"Where is she anyway?" Ledger asks. He's chewing his food too much. An eating disorder fucked with his mind as a teenager. He thinks I don't know. But I found the bills for that fancy outpatient treatment center Dad helped him get into. All this time, everyone thought he went to basketball camp for a few hours each day.

"With Chloe. They went into town." Chloe said something about needing yarn for her latest project. Apparently, she knits Christmas gifts. I want to ask her who the scarves are for. I want to know why she's knitting so many pairs of mittens. Of course, I don't ask. I barely say anything.

It's been a week and she's settling in. Her clothes are all over my living room couch. Her shoes, keys, and wallet are scattered on my kitchen island. Her reading tablet and planner are on the coffee table. I shouldn't love all those little things so much, but I do.

I'm already dreading next week when I'll be away from her and Abby. I have to go out of town for ranch business. One of our suppliers wants a face-to-face meeting.

The only good thing about all the traveling I do is the opportunity to meet homeless teens. I always buy them a hot meal and give them a card for the ranch, invite them down to Courage County if they ever get out that way.

I remember when being on the streets was better than being in the home the system had placed me in. I'm a long way from that kid but I've never forgotten. It's why I can't let Abby go into the system. I'll die before I let her grow up the way I did.

"Chloe is cute," Ledger says. "I was thinking of asking her out."

"They'd never find your body." My voice is quiet and steely, filled with conviction. Ledger is a good guy. He'd treat her right. But nobody gets to spend time with my woman. Not even my brother.

West reaches into his wallet and passes Ledger a crisp twenty. "You were right."

"See? Crazy for her." He pockets the bill and faces me. "What are you doing about it, moron?"

I ball up the rest of my sandwich in my wrapper, my appetite suddenly gone. My teeth ache with how badly I want Chloe. But that doesn't make what I feel right. It's never been right and I'm man enough to admit that. "Chloe is young, and she's my employee."

"When you love someone, you should go after her," Ledger says as if he's some damn expert on the topic of love and relationships.

"Yeah, and when was the last time you told Peyton that you love her?" I challenge. It's a low blow and we all know it. Maybe I should be fuckin' sensitive or something. He's been in love with her since they were teenagers and for whatever reason, they both keep dancing around the truth. Neither will admit just how much they want to cross that line and be a real couple. Hell, maybe it's some twisted game that I don't understand.

He flinches. "I'm planning on it."

Yeah, he's been planning on it for years. West and I both know he's not going to do it. The moment he admits his feelings to her, she's going to pack up everything she owns and run away. Problem is, I'm not sure Ledger will recover from that heartache. They're soulmates.

"Ledger is right." West's voice carries a hard edge. He's protective over Ledger. We both are. We know he had it tough growing up. Then dealing with his mental health. Can't be easy to live with all that shit.

I glance his way, feeling guilty for what I said. "It was a dick thing to say."

He shrugs, and I know it's forgiven. That's Ledger though. The man has never held a grudge against anyone. If there were anyone worthy of sainthood, it'd probably be him.

"Do you know how long I wasted not being with Cassie?" West asks. "A decade. A decade when we could have been building a life together. But I was an idiot who kept his feelings to himself."

I glare at him. I might be OK that my sister's getting married. But I'm still not crazy about the idea, given that I walked in on them a few days ago. Add that one to the list of things that have scarred me for life.

"I'm too old for her," I mumble. There's no way she looks at me and feels anything. This whole thing is something I've created in my head to deal with the truth that's getting harder to push down. I'm lonely. I want someone to share a life with. I want a woman to grow old with me as we raise Abby together. Maybe add a few more little ones to the brood.

"Ask her to the Christmas dance tonight. See if she accepts," Ledger says.

West is quick to add, "You won't know if you don't at least try."

They're being ridiculous, and I shake my head. No way am I going to follow their crap advice and lose my nanny.

Chloe

"Yeah, I'm doing good, Mama," I tell her as I juggle the car seat and my purse to get back into Micah's office. I've been running errands with Abby all morning. She still sleeps a lot but I'm certain that she's becoming a little more aware of her surroundings. I could almost swear she smiled at me this morning.

"Your new boss treating you right?" She demands. I can almost see her at the kitchen counter, peeling potatoes for supper. I can smell the dirt and earth, hear my siblings playing at her feet as she works, and the way she has her cookbook with the crinkled pages open and turned to the roasted garlic mashed potatoes recipe. Not that she ever bothers to consult it. She knows every recipe in that book by heart.

A wave of homesickness overwhelms me at the memories. I remind myself that I'm happy here with Abby and Micah.

I love her. I love her fussiness and the way it frustrates Micah that he can't find a way to comfort her. I love the way he tries to make funny faces to entertain her and that he gets up every night to sit with her when she cries. Even when it's my night, he won't leave her alone. I think maybe he's one of those men who's meant to be a father. Unlike my own.

"He's nice, Mama," I tell her, trying not to think of the Christmas dance that's happening tonight. It's all anyone was talking about when I went into town.

I kept wondering what it would be like if Micah asked me. It's a silly fantasy.

Something in my tone must have tipped off Mama because she sighs. The sound is long-suffering. "Don't go getting ideas about him."

"I won't," I answer as I unbuckle Abby from her seat. I give her a quick diaper change while we continue to talk. "He's an amazing father though."

"Yeah, well, you start thinking like that and next thing you know you've got eight little mouths to feed," she says. It's hard to fault her for being bitter. She's had a hard life. Her first husband, my dad, abandoned her. Number two was abusive. Number three cheated on her. Each man took a little more of her light until she was only left with a pile of bills and a lot of hungry kids.

I won't make that mistake, I promise myself. To distract my mom, I start telling her about the online college courses I'm taking. Right now, I'm getting the basics out of the way. But eventually, I plan to go to nursing school. I'll make a nice hourly rate when I graduate. My mama won't have to struggle anymore. There will finally be enough groceries and the light bill will be paid on time.

Once my call with my mom is over, I breathe a sigh of relief. The small crush I have on Micah isn't a big deal. He's hardly ever around me. In fact, he seems to go out of his way to limit the amount of time we spend together. I shouldn't take it personally, but it hurts a little bit.

Abby coos. I can't tell if she's cooing at me, but I echo the noise anyway. Mama always said it's their first conversations.

"Are you ready to decorate for Christmas with me, sweet girl?" I ask as I reach for my shopping bags. I found a few items at the craft store that would be perfect for Micah's office. It's strange to me. His house is decorated for the holiday, but his work area isn't. Seems like he could use some Christmas cheer in here.

For the next twenty minutes, I narrate every decorating decision to Abby. Whenever she makes a noise, I respond and agree with her.

"And I think we're done," I tell her as I step back and admire my work. There's a tiny Christmas tree that sparkles and shimmers on Micah's desk, and I hung some garland around the front of it. Plus, there are twinkle lights around the door now. And yeah, maybe I hung a little bit of mistletoe.

Abby looks around in wonder, and I point to the mistletoe. "See? This is what you do with mistletoe."

I press a quick kiss to her cheek just as the door swings open.

Micah stomps his boots on the rug and stumbles in with a blast of cold air. He glances around the office and for the first time since I started my little decorating spree, I wonder if it was a bad idea. "I thought Abby would like it. I can take it all down."

He doesn't answer. Instead, he stalks across the floor until he's standing in front of me, boot to boot. His gaze searches my face, but I don't know what he's hoping to find there.

My heart rate speeds up, and I lick my suddenly dry lips. "Do you hate it?"

"I can't hate anything you do," he murmurs before he lowers his head and presses his lips to mine.

The kiss is sweet and gentle. At least until I open my mouth to his tongue, then everything changes. His hand goes to my hip, the other cradles my head. He presses his body as close to mine as he can, making little growls in the back of his throat. His noises break my trance and bring me back to the present. That's when I realize what I'm doing. I'm kissing my boss. My much older, very sexy boss.

4
MICAH

Chloe's pupils are blown wide, and she's breathing hard. The cutest blush is covering her cheeks right now, and all I want to do is grab her and keep kissing her. Then I want to take her back to my house and spend the rest of my life making love to her. They don't really need me here to run the ranch. Surely, one of my brothers would figure things out eventually.

Abby coos between us, as if she's reminding me that she's still here. But that only fuels my fantasies. Chloe and I having more babies together, building a beautiful family right there in my place.

"Micah," she whispers my name and presses a hand against of one of her hot cheeks.

Yeah, maybe I'm getting ahead of myself. But I know forever when I see it and Chloe is definitely my forever. I just have to figure out a way to tell her without freaking her out. So, I blurt out the only thing I can think of, "Go to the Christmas dance with me."

What I really want to tell her is to marry me, but I hold my tongue. Fuck, is this how West felt about Cassie for ten years? Is this why he looks at her like she's the one who paints every sunset?

"That...You didn't ask me."

I blink, the thought having never occurred to me. "Why would I ask?"

"That's what a man does for a date."

"Maybe weak men who would be happy letting you slip through their fingers," I answer. She's mine. Doesn't she know that? Can't she feel it just from that one kiss? We're meant to be. It's inevitable, and I'm not letting her run from this.

She chuckles at that and carries Abby across the room to the playpen. She sets her down in it, giving me a view of the most perfect ass that's ever been around. My pants grow tighter as I imagine her bent across my bed like that with me plowing into her from behind. Now that I know she feels something for me, every depraved and filthy fantasy that I've tried to fight against is rushing forward.

She straightens and turns around. She quirks an eyebrow when she realizes where my eyes were. "Yes, I'll go to the Christmas dance with you." She pauses then and chews on her lip. "Except I don't have anything to wear."

All the better. We'll stay at my place and have our own private Christmas dance. I definitely think I'll like that better. Still, I'm thinking I shouldn't share that idea out loud. "Go into town and get one. Expense it to the ranch."

She frowns. "I can't do that."

"Yeah, I'll write the whole evening off as an expense," I answer. Truth is, there are a lot of expenses for the ranch that I never claim. To me, it's silly to get reimbursed when it's a family business. But if she wants a pretty dress—if she wants a million of them—I'll happily make sure she gets them. "I do a lot of business at these events."

"Abby needs a bottle first."

"Go ahead and feed her. I'll take care of everything," I promise. This will be an evening neither of us forget.

Chloe

Micah wasn't lying when he said he'd take care of everything. While I was feeding Abby, he stepped outside to make a phone call. Next thing I know, Cassie showed up with a ranch credit card and squealing that we were going to have so much fun.

"We have to make a quick pit stop," she tells me, pulling her tiny silver car into the apartment complex in town. "Have you ever been inside Liquid Courage?"

I shake my head. I work too damn hard for my paychecks to be the type that drinks them away. At least, that's how I used to feel. Now I get to spend my days taking care of my little Abby. It's still hard but it doesn't feel like work. It just feels like I was meant to be doing it.

"Well, this is Peyton. She's the bartender there and she's..." Cassie pauses and presses her lips together. Finally, she adds, "Ledger's best friend."

"Are they not best friends anymore?" I ask, trying to understand her hesitation.

"Oh, they're best friends," she answers too quickly.

Before I can ask anything else, Peyton is

bounding into the backseat of the car. Her enthusiasm and energy surprise me. She's covered in tattoos and when she talks, I can see something in her mouth shine. It takes me a second to realize it's a tongue ring. "This is perfect. I need a girls' day out."

Despite the fact that I barely know Peyton and Cassie, the three of us fall into an easy rhythm while clothes shopping. They help me select a purple dress with a deep V in the back.

Cassie claps her hands together. "My brother is going to flip when he sees you in this."

"It's perfect," Peyton agrees. We talked her into a ruby red dress with a slit up the thigh. I think she's going with Ledger to the dance. I'm curious about their relationship but I don't know how to ask. Even if I did, it's not my business to pry.

"Are you going to the dance?" I ask Cassie.

"Already got my dress, though I don't think West will let me wear it for long. He's such a caveman." But her tone is filled with amusement and something else. Lust and longing and love.

I think about my mom and the way she's been through so much with the men she's married. "How did you know West was the one for you?"

A dreamy smile takes over Cassie's face. "I always

knew he was the one, from the first moment I saw him."

"You didn't. No one finds their soulmate as a teenager." Peyton snorts. But the look on her face isn't one of disbelief. It's envy. She quickly hides it when she realizes I'm looking at her.

Cassie doesn't seem the least bit bothered by Peyton's words. If anything, she lets out a soft sigh.

I half expect singing woodland creatures to appear and her to break into song. From everything I've heard, West and Cassie are practically a fairytale, except for the ten year wait and all. "I was scared, and he didn't think I returned his feelings. Love is complicated sometimes."

"That's silly," Peyton insists. "If he really felt something for you all that time, he would have stepped up and told you. Guys don't hide their feelings and pine for a woman for years."

That's when I remember Cassie's hesitation to define Peyton's relationship with Ledger in the car. There's something more beneath the surface. Is Peyton in love with Ledger? Does he return her feelings, or has he hidden his so well that she doesn't even know?

Cassie puts her hand on Peyton's shoulder and

gives it a firm squeeze. "They do if they don't think you return them."

Peyton shakes her head and looks away but not before I see the sheen of tears in them. She blinks and her voice wobbles when she says, "Let's get dressed again. I'll spring for burgers at Ernie's."

I quickly agree to burgers and retreat to my dressing room. I've longed for Micah for a few weeks while Cassie and Peyton have been in love with their cowboys for years. I can't imagine what kind of pain they both carried. Cassie got her happy ending with West. Maybe in time, Peyton and Ledger will find their way to each other.

Inside the diner is crowded and noisy and for a second, I panic when Abby isn't with me. I'm so used to having her in my arms or beside me in her car seat. It feels weird to be without her and it surprises me how much I miss her. She's definitely not a job to me. She feels like a piece of my heart that's always been missing. So does her father. The realization should scare me, but it doesn't. Maybe because everything with Micah feels so right.

As soon as we're settled with our food, Peyton asks about Cassie's wedding plans. Apparently, she and West are getting married on Christmas Eve. I listen to the two of them talking, wondering the entire time why some marriages make it, and some don't. Why some men are good and true and will sacrifice everything for their families while others are content to let their wives and kids live in poverty and violence and drunkenness.

Micah doesn't strike me as that kind of guy. He's given everything to make the ranch a success. No matter how tired he is when he comes home every day, he still takes time to make silly faces with Abby before asking me what I want for dinner and cooking. He'd even do the dishes afterward if I didn't shoo him away and insist he go take some time to relax.

"Have you and West talked about where you're going for the honeymoon?" Peyton asks.

Cassie's already flushed cheeks darken to an even deeper shade of pink. "He's taking me to this beautiful ski lodge in Colorado."

I dip my fry in the special sauce Ernie makes and pop it into my mouth. "That'll be fun. I've never been skiing."

Peyton laughs from her spot in the booth beside me. "I don't think she's going to be doing much skiing."

Cassie wiggles her eyebrows. "If all goes according to plan, definitely not."

Oh, shit. I just realized I was imagining a very different kind of honeymoon. I wonder what a honeymoon with Micah would be like and instantly, I feel hot all over. I wonder if he'd be just as growly in bed as he is when he's marching around the ranch, bossing people around. Would he put my hands above my head and insist that I'm his? Would he feast on me for hours, not letting me up until I'd orgasmed again and again? Would I finally get to see his big cock? Would he be disappointed by my inexperience?

"You and West have only been together for a little while, right?" I ask softly, keeping my gaze on the chipped table. I don't want my thoughts showing on my face.

"Not even a month officially," she says.

"And did you...Were you..." This has to be the most embarrassing question in the history of the universe. But I have to know. "Compatible, you know...in the bedroom?"

She chuckles. "I have no complaints and neither does he."

I keep my voice quiet, not wanting it to carry in

the restaurant. "But you were alike in the experience department?"

"I don't follow," she says.

I finally force myself to look at her. "I'm not. I don't. I'm...you know." I've never been ashamed of being a virgin. But what if it's a turn-off for Micah?

Beside me, Peyton sends Cassie a look. Finally, understanding crosses her expression and I could hug Peyton because I'm so grateful she didn't make me say it out loud in this crowded diner.

"He just seems a lot more experienced than me," I offer. What was Abby's mom like? Were they in love when they got together? He never talks about her, and it worries me. What will he tell Abby one day when she's older?

"I thought that about West," she says. "I thought there'd be this huge gap and there wasn't much of one at all. And I really don't want to be thinking about my brother like that. But come on, the man eats the same thing for dinner every night and still buys the same brand of toothpaste that he did when we were teenagers. He's not likely to have...*experience* with lots of women."

I blow out a breath, my stomach still tight. "I know that. It's just, I really like him, Cassie. Like rearrange your whole life plans like him. Like seeing your entire future differently. Like wanting to dream new dreams, dreams that scare you."

"You're in love with him," Peyton says.

As soon as she says the words, the rightness of it hits me. I am in love with Micah Kringle, and I don't know if the thought should terrify or delight me. All I know is it's too late to protect my heart now.

5
CHLOE

"Mom, Mom. We don't need pictures. This isn't a high school dance," Micah tells his mom. Not that it's stopping her. She's insisting on taking photos of everyone together. Cassie, Peyton, and I got ready at his parents' house with Mrs. Kringle clucking over us the entire time. From hairpins to clear fashion tape, the woman thought of everything.

Now we're all in the living room along with our dates for the evening. The whole space feels crowded with so many of us here. Mr. Kringle is even here. He's in a recliner in the living room and he's baby talking with Abby. He's clearly enamored with his granddaughter and not for the first time, I wish I had a big extended family. A lot of people who surrounded me with love and affection. What would my life have been like growing up if it hadn't been just Mom and my siblings?

Mrs. Kringle pulls down the camera which is trained on me and scowls at her son. "You never went to any of the dances. I have no pictures of my son all dressed up and taking a pretty girl out to a dance." She points to the fireplace mantle where she has photos of a young Ledger with Peyton on his arm and West with a very young, flushed Cassie smiling up at him adoringly. "Now, Micah Jonathan Kringle, you can give me one phony smile for the cameras."

He scowls back at her but it's obvious from his expression that he adores her. I'm pretty sure he's going to give her whatever she wants. He sends her flowers every week. A pretty wildflower bouquet that sits on her kitchen counter. That's just one of the many things she told me about her son while I was getting ready. The woman is an encyclopedia on him. But I noticed there weren't any stories from before he was a teenager. It makes me think he was adopted late in life and that makes me sad for him.

"I never went to any of my school dances either," I tell Micah.

He finally relents. "One photo, Ma. Just one."

"Come on, give the woman what she wants, and

we'll be out of here faster," Ledger tells Micah. He has his arm around Peyton's hip in a possessive gesture. She said he's been acting weird all night, ever since he saw her in that dress.

"Five more minutes, Mom," West warns. He's been looking at Cassie like he's about to call this whole thing off, take her back to their home, and tear that dress from her body.

"Now just one group shot and one of you together and one..." His mom continues talking, but I can't pay attention to her anymore. Micah has squeezed next to me for the group photo.

"Sorry about this," he murmurs in my ear, his breath hot against the skin of my neck.

I fight a shiver at his nearness. Can the rest of his family tell how much he affects me? Can they sense the feelings I have for him? I've been trying so hard to maintain my poker face around everyone.

My fingers find his, and I give his hand a little squeeze. "I like it."

His posture relaxes. Was he worried about his family embarrassing me? I don't ever want him thinking that I don't care for his big, overbearing family. "I like them too."

"I like you," he murmurs right before he brushes a kiss across my lips.

"No making out like horny teenagers in my house," Mr. Kringle calls.

Micah pulls away from our kiss and glares in his father's direction. "Dad! Don't use that word in front of my daughter."

He beams down at her. "She doesn't know what any of it means, do you, princess?"

After a flurry of pictures from Mrs. Kringle, it's finally time to leave.

"Maybe she should come with us," I tell Micah when I see the way he's looking at Abby. He's clearly torn about leaving her behind. He leaves her under my care all the time but I'm usually hanging out in the office with him or at home with him. Yeah, he's busy handling work or dealing with household responsibilities, but she's always nearby.

"Nonsense," Mr. Kringle insists. "I was promised a night with my granddaughter, and I'm going to take advantage of it. You can see her again in a few hours."

"She'll be fine, Micah," Mrs. Kringle says, ushering us toward the door. The others have already left but it's different for Micah. Half of his heart is staying behind.

I tug on his hand, pulling him onto the porch. It's hard for me too. But he'll have to trust her with them eventually. After all, I want a lot more dates with my man in the future.

"OK, but call me if she gets upset or spits up. Sometimes, she does this thing where she starts to spit up and you think it's over but then it keeps coming. If that happens, her tummy gets—"

Mrs. Kringle closes the door in his face, ending his lecture.

He scowls at the door for a moment before turning his attention to me. "You think they'll call?"

"They'll call you if there's a problem," I reassure him. I press a kiss to his lips to distract him. I meant for it to be a quick, chaste peck. But the moment our lips connect, Micah is deepening the kiss. He runs his tongue along my bottom lip, nipping until I give him access. His tongue explores my mouth, stroking gently until suddenly he's stopping.

Mr. Kringle is standing there with Abby in his arms. "You're giving the neighbors a show."

"We don't have neighbors," Micah protests.

"You still can't maul her like an animal on my porch. At least get her to the dance, son."

I chuckle even though my cheeks are warm. I do feel like a teenager when I'm around Micah, but in a good way. In that crazy can't-keep-my-hands-off-of-him type of way. If his kiss was any indication, Micah feels the exact same.

We say goodnight again to his father, and Micah puts a hand on my back as he leads me toward his truck. My skin is cold with so little material but it's worth it for the feeling of his hand on me. Before he opens the door, he shrugs out of his suitcoat.

I wrap myself in it, loving both the smell of his cologne and his warmth. He makes me feel so safe and cared for. Is this how love is supposed to be? Does it go cold to wrap you in warmth?

As soon as we're in the truck, Micah's hand finds mine. The way his big hand engulfs mine makes me feel tiny and protected. I think this man would do anything for me, and I'm certain I'd do the same.

"Can I ask you something?" I'm toasty warm since he aimed all the heaters at me. But I still don't want to give up his jacket. It's nice wearing something that was on his body. "Where is Abby's mama?"

Micah

SHE ASKED THE ONE QUESTION I DON'T KNOW HOW TO answer. I wish I had something to give her. Something to give my daughter because one day, she'll ask me that same question. The thought that I won't have an answer or that worse, she'll think that it somehow means she's worthless leaves me wanting to howl with rage. How do I explain to the most perfect little girl in the world that she wasn't wanted?

The miles pass in silence, and Chloe doesn't push. Of course, she doesn't. She's never been anything less than kind and understanding. But we can't move forward if I don't answer these questions. We'll be forever stuck in this awkward dance, neither of us quite sure where we stand.

"I'm not sure where she is," I finally confess. What kind of father doesn't know where his daughter's mother is? Why don't I know?

I spend hours every night online, combing through social media posts and forums. I'm looking for clues, something that will tell me who she is and why she gave up her sweet little baby. Something that will tell me where she is and if she needs help. Fuck, I hope she's not in trouble.

I've considered every possibility. Is my Abby the product of an assault? Was she born to a woman facing domestic violence? What made her choose me? How does she know my name? Have we ever met?

"Were you...close with her?"

"No," I admit. I mean, I couldn't have been. It's not like I'm spending my time around pregnant women. I work the ranch and occasionally, I help out a homeless teen. But that's it.

"So, you never loved her?"

The question nearly breaks me. I can't figure out how to explain this. If she ever comes back and wants Abby, could I fight her? Would I have any legal grounds? Or would what I've done be considered kidnapping? I'm pretty sure you're not allowed to do finders keepers with a baby, even if someone left her on your porch. Would all of this make Chloe an accessory?

I tighten my hold on the steering wheel at the thought. I can't risk that. I can't tell her everything and implicate her. "No. It's hard to explain and complicated."

"But it's over now?" I don't like the hesitation in her tone. I don't like the idea that she doesn't know where she stands with me.

I squeeze her fingers, applying gentle pressure to her small hands. "There's nothing between Abby's mom and me. You're the only woman I want in my life and my bed."

She chuckles softly. "You haven't gotten me there yet."

"Give it time," I murmur, pressing my lips to her fingertips. Being with Chloe is the most natural thing in the world. Dad always said that when the right woman comes along, you know it. I always thought he was full of smoke but now I get it. Because the moment I saw Chloe, everything in my life shifted. She became mine and only mine. My heart beats for her. For her and little Abby.

I stop the truck in the parking lot of the community center and help her inside. Before I can get her on the dance floor, we're stopped by so many of the townsfolk. All of them want to make small talk, and I force myself to be polite when I want to drag Chloe onto the dance floor and hold her in my arms.

After I've finally managed to excuse us from a conversation with Mayor Banks, I pull her into my embrace. My fingertips touch her back and fuck, her skin is so soft. Is it this soft everywhere? What's on underneath this? Because I'm not seeing a bra line, and I definitely shouldn't be thinking about that when I'm surrounded by all of these fine people.

My voice is a deep, rasping growl in her ear that I

barely recognize, "Did I tell you just how damn sexy you are?"

"You didn't," she says softly.

Did I really do that? Did I not take a moment to appreciate just how incredibly beautiful she is and let her know that? Never again, I vow to myself. Never again will I let a day pass without reminding her of how beautiful and sexy she is.

"Well, you are, and that dress is making my cock hard." To emphasize the point, I grind my hips against her. Not enough to be indecent right here in the community center. But enough that her eyes widen.

"Yeah, that's all for you, sweetheart. All nine inches," I promise.

"Micah! You can't say stuff like that." No outrage colors her tone. Her nipples are hard points against my chest, and every time I move, she tilts her pelvis. She's trying to carefully grind against me. It's just dark enough in here that no one would notice, not unless they were looking directly at us. Besides, all the couples are lost in their own little worlds, oblivious to the nasty things I'm whispering in my woman's ear.

I press kisses along her jaw before I nip at her earlobe. Her skin smells amazing. It's a mix of vanilla and jasmine. At first, I thought it was her perfume. But after spending the last week with her, I recognize that it's just her sweet scent, something unique to Chloe. "Are you aching? Is that pretty little pussy of yours hurting?"

She groans. "Please."

That one word nearly undoes me. My cock pushes painfully against my zipper. "You want me to take care of you right here?"

"Yes." The word is a breathy whimper, letting me know she's too far gone to care about where we are. Fuck, I'm too far gone too. But her sounds will be for my ears only.

Taking her hand, I pull her away from the dance floor. I stick to the dark corners at the edge of the room so no one will try to talk with us. I thread my way to the back of the community center where the women's bathroom is unlocked.

Fortunately, the stalls are empty, and the settee covered in a pastel print from the sixties is just heavy enough. I give it a harsh shove and it slides behind the door. Yeah, nobody is coming through there anytime soon.

"What are you doing?" She asks, watching me.

I stalk toward her, a hunter spotting prey. "Fucking my girl."

6
MICAH

Her eyes grow wide, and she licks her dry lips. "There's, uh, something you should probably know."

I don't stop prowling toward her. There's nothing she could say that would make me want her less. As it is, I feel like I'm on the edge of combusting. My dick is leaking in my pants, and all I want is to touch her. To feast on her, to know every inch of her skin.

"I'm…inexperienced," she finally finishes right as I stand in front of her.

I didn't expect that. A girl as beautiful as my Chloe surely had dozens of opportunities. The boys around her couldn't have been that blind. "And that's a big deal?"

"Well, I don't know if it is to you." She bites her bottom lip.

Maybe this is the point I should tell her that I'm also inexperienced but she's already nervous. I'm not about to make her more nervous so I do the one thing I've been doing since I was a kid just trying to survive the system. I take control. Picking her up in my arms bridal style, it feels so perfect to be holding her. Like she was born to be right here.

I cross the bathroom and set her carefully on the opposite settee, the one that's not against the door. I drop to my knees on the tile floor, not giving a damn about my dress pants. Only one thing on my mind right now. "First things first, I'm gonna lick this pretty little cherry. Then I'm going to claim it."

She squeezes her thighs together and whispers a soft, "OK."

That's all the permission I need. "Lean back, sweetheart."

She does as I said, relaxing into the cushions. The absolute trust in her eyes about guts me. I promise here and now to always be worthy of it. To be worthy of her.

"Spread these thighs for me." After weeks of wanting this woman—craving her night and day—

she's finally here with me. Finally letting me see this sweet pussy.

I reach for her foot slinging her leg over my shoulder, so she'll be completely open to me. Nothing I want hidden from my view. Chloe is my girl and there are no secrets between us. "You know how long I've been dreaming about this, fucking my hand to thoughts of you? Weeks."

"W-weeks?" She repeats, sounding dazed.

"Since the first moment I saw you standing there in Emma May's store," I admit as I bunch up the hem of her dress. I shove it high on her thighs and let my fingertips ghost along her soft, satiny skin. The pretty panties she's wearing are a soft lilac color and there's an obvious wet spot on the front of them. The sight of it makes me want to beat on my chest in feral pride.

My cock is so hard that I'm pretty sure my balls are going to explode. But there's nothing that could move me from this spot right now. My woman needs me to cure her ache and as her man, it's my damn privilege to be the one who takes care of her.

"Me, too."

I draw little circles on her thighs with my thumbs and pause to look at her. No matter how long this takes, I will put her first. I'll make sure she comes again and again.

She seems to realize I don't understand because she explains, "Since the first moment I saw you, I've thought of you too."

The breath leaves my lungs in a whoosh. "Did you touch yourself while thinking about me?"

She bites her lip again and gives me a shy nod. She's fucked herself to thoughts of me, wondered about these moments between us. The knowledge makes me feel like a damn superhero.

"You thought about how I would touch you? What I would say? Where we'd be?"

"You always said d-dirty things," she admits.

I bury my face against the wet material between her legs. "Did I tell you how good your pussy smells? Because it smells fuckin' divine, like a treat that's all for me."

Then, because I can't help myself, I lick her through the damp material. Her answering gasp is all the confirmation I need that I'm on the right track. I play with her pussy through her panties and grind against the edge of the furniture. It doesn't do much to resolve my ache, especially when she's squirming like that.

She moans my name and thrusts her pussy

deeper into my face. That's when I hook a finger around the gusset of her panties and move them aside. The sight that greets me has my balls drawing even tighter. She's so pink and puffy and glistening.

My first taste of her skin with no barriers between us has me groaning. She tastes just like she smells, sweet and tart. A treat I'll always crave.

Despite the way my own body is aching, I take my time. I lick her slowly, concentrating my strokes on everywhere except that little nub that's peeking out from her hood. I'm desperate to play with it but not until I've opened her. She'll take my cock soon and I need to know she'll be ready.

Slipping a finger into her channel, I listen to her noises to tell me if she's still enjoying this. Her little gasps and mewls confirm I'm on the right track. I keep teasing her with my tongue, making sure to touch her with it everywhere except the place she wants it the most.

Finally, when her wet channel starts to open to me, I squeeze in another finger. It's a tight fit and I have to pause long enough to count backwards. Otherwise, I'm going to come right here in my pants like the horny bastard I am.

"Micah," she moans my name.

I look up at her then. She's so damn beautiful

with her legs slung over my shoulders while she rides my face like the queen she is. My face will always be her throne and I'll make sure she takes her place on it daily for the rest of our lives.

"You want to come?" I murmur, crooking my fingers. I've heard a rumor that there's a place and judging by the pleasure that just flickered across her face, I think I found it. I rub the area again only this time I lean forward and lick her slit. I tongue that beautiful pearl, and she shatters on the spot. She whispers my name with such devotion that it sounds like a holy chant. It's the most beautiful sound in the world.

I eat her through the high, not caring that she squirts all over my face and into my beard. I'll wear her juices everyday just to let the rest of the world know who I belong to. To let every man know that I'm the one who pleases my queen. Who satisfies her so thoroughly.

As her shudders ease and she floats back down, she gives me a sated grin. "That was...I've never..."

"I know," I whisper and press a soft kiss to her lips. She's perfect and she's mine in every way.

She reaches for my belt then, her fingers fumbling with the buckle. Her hands are shaking so I put my hand over hers. "We can wait."

Impatience crosses her features. "I don't want to wait."

"You want your first time here, in the community center bathroom?" I scowl down at her. She deserves better than this. She deserves my big king-size bed with roses and candles and soft music.

"I want my first time with you. Where we are doesn't matter, and dammit, you promised me."

I search her face, making sure she's certain. I don't ever want her to regret our first union. It would crush me to know she ever had regrets about us.

"I know what I want," she whispers as she presses a kiss to my still damp face. But it's when she presses her lips to mine and sucks on my tongue, I know I'm too far gone.

"Lean back," I growl at her and help her stretch out on the settee. She hikes her dress up and works her panties down her legs until they drop onto the floor. The caveman can't resist; I grab them and shove them into my pocket for later. Yeah, I'll be working my cock to her smell. I'll always crave it. Always want her.

Reaching for my belt, I manage to work my pants far enough down my thighs that my cock springs free. He's already ready for her, the greedy bastard slick with moisture. I pump him twice while I eye her swollen pussy. "Tell me it's all for me. Ask me to wreck this sweet cunt."

Her cheeks flush but then she repeats the dirty words.

It's nearly my undoing to hear such filthy things fall from her lips.

"Micah," she nearly sobs as I align our bodies and touch her clit.

"I know, baby." I thrust inside in one smooth motion. But I still at her shudder. Her breathing turns shallow for a moment, and I reach out to cup her cheek. She's the most precious thing in the world to me. "Take your time. Tell me when it starts to feel better."

"It's...already fading."

I still hold out, fighting every instinct that demands I plow into her. This sweet pussy is gripping me so well and all I want is to ram her full.

"Ooh." The tension finally bleeds from her muscles, and I feel the exact moment her pussy adjusts to my monster girth. "Maybe try now."

I experiment with a short thrust, making sure to roll my hips, so her clit gets some friction too. "Better?"

She makes a little noise of contentment and

meets my next thrust, lifting her hips for it. Together, our bodies find a slow, sweaty rhythm. But it's not just the physical sensations that feels so good. It's staring down into Chloe's sweet gaze. It's knowing that my body is bringing her pleasure. I'm still cupping her cheek, and I want more than anything to tell her. I want to whisper those three words and have her know the truth of them.

But I'm pretty sure a man isn't supposed to say it for the first time when he's balls deep. So instead of saying it, I focus on showing her. Giving her every ounce of pleasure that my body has to share with her.

I feel it, the moment she starts to come. Her pussy milks my cock so tightly that I can't hold back anymore. I shoot my release deep into her womb and even though this is still new, I put my forehead against hers and send up a silent prayer that we'll get forever together.

7
CHLOE

"Do you think everyone can tell?" I ask as I stare at my reflection in the bathroom mirror. Micah's arms are around me, his front pressed to my back. After we made love, he helped set my clothes to right and we both washed our hands. I was about to go back out. But he stopped, told me to let him hold me for a minute.

I know that losing your virginity doesn't change you. But I feel so different. My blood is buzzing, and my hair is messy and more than that, I know for certain that I'm in love with the gruff cowboy who's holding onto me so tenderly.

"Tell what?" He presses a soft kiss to my shoulder.

"That we...you know."

"That I just ate your sweet pussy in the community center bathroom?" He arches an eyebrow. "Or that I made you come so hard you saw stars while I was buried deep in your cunt?"

"Micah," I call his name in reproach. But his filthy words bring my body to life again. I'm already aching for him. I need a thousand more nights like tonight. I need to spend endless hours together exploring each other. "Take me home."

His eyes darken and his voice is strangled when he asks, "Won't you miss the rest of the dance?"

"It's an annual thing," I remind him. It's not like the Christmas dance won't be here next year and the year after that. Courage County loves its traditions, especially the holiday ones.

"That's a good point," he agrees and quickly tugs me from the bathroom.

It takes a century to get back out to the truck. Everyone wants to talk to Micah. It's clear they all respect him. More than that, they adore him if the affectionate pats and hugs are anything to go by. He's beloved in this town and it makes me happy that this community has his back. Still, it's hard to concentrate when he's tracing circles with his thumb on my back as he talks.

If this keeps up, I might just explode right here.

That would certainly make the front page of the newspaper.

As soon as we're in the truck, he puts an arm around my hip and slides me into the middle. It's an awkward fit around the gear shift but I don't complain. I like being snuggled close to him as he drives us back home.

"My parents offered to keep Abby for the evening," he says softly when he's paused at one of the few stoplights in town.

I know he must be making the offer for me. There's no way he wants to be apart from her for a whole night and neither do I. "Micah Kringle, you go get our daughter."

He turns to look at me, the light adding red highlights to his dark hair. "Our daughter?"

I didn't even realize I'd called her that. I don't know when I started thinking about Abby as my daughter and our daughter, but I can't deny the rightness of it. I nod decisively. "Our daughter."

He squeezes my hip and repeats it under his breath, a smile playing at his lips. "We're a family."

"Yeah, I guess we are." I chuckle at the thought. Sometimes, family is the people you're born to and sometimes, it's the people around you, the ones you choose.

The entire drive back to his parents' place, Micah and I keep looking at each other and smiling. I know we're picking Abby up too early because I can see the disappointment on Mr. Kringle's face.

"We'll let you keep her overnight next time," I promise.

He brightens at my words and glances at Micah. He's busy with his mom. They're putting Abby in her car seat and he's asking a million questions about what she did tonight. I'm kind of surprised he hasn't demanded his mom submit a five-page written report.

Mr. Kringle leans in close. His white, bushy eyebrows come together when he says, "He likes you."

I think back to tonight in the bathroom and the dirty things my cowboy said to me. "I think you might be right."

"He doesn't show much. Still waters run deep. Remember that with him."

I start to dismiss his concerns. But then I wonder if one day I'll be giving this same warning to Abby's future boyfriend. So instead, I say, "He's an amazing man. Thank you for giving him to me."

He beams at me, and I can't help feeling like I passed some test I didn't even realize I was taking.

He claps his hand on my shoulder. "Welcome to the family, Chloe."

My eyes fill with tears that I have to blink back. I hadn't considered that when I chose Micah and Abby, I was also choosing his parents. I guess that's how love works. His family becomes yours and yours become his. Will he want to meet my mama one day? Or visit with my little siblings?

I'm quiet on the three-mile drive to Micah's place. He's the one who lives closest to the Kringles. He may not have been born to them but it's clear that he is their son in every way. I'm still quiet as Micah gives Abby her usual bath and sings her a lullaby.

"You all right?" He asks with an arm around my shoulders. We're standing over the crib, watching the world's most beautiful little girl drift to sleep. Do babies dream? If they do, I hope hers are always pleasant and filled with the sweetest images.

"She's perfect," I whisper, overwhelmed with awe and wonder. Will I carry my own children one day? It's not like Micah and I used protection tonight. The thought should worry me, but it doesn't. Because despite everything in my past, I know we're going to be together forever.

"I'm afraid she's going to be taken from me."

I glance at his face.

He blows out a breath. "I mean, it has something to do with being a foster kid. Getting ripped away from whichever home I was in that week or month. It's always in the back of my mind. That one day, I'm going to lose everyone I love. That I'll wake up and they'll just be gone."

I put my hand on his chest, feeling the steady thrum of his heartbeat beneath the material of his dress shirt. "But it's worse with Abby for some reason."

He searches my face. Whatever he sees on it must reassure him because he says, "She's not mine."

I look between him and the crib, trying to work out what he means by that. They adore each other, that much is clear. Babies know when they're loved and wanted.

"She just showed up on my doorstep one day with a note."

"Are you sure she's not yours?" I ask, my stomach sinking at his confession. "Maybe it was a drunken thing you forgot about. That stuff happens sometimes. You may not even remember her name."

He shakes his head. "Tonight was my first."

"Your first what?" It takes my brain a moment to

catch up, then I can't help the smile that stretches across my face. "Really?"

He shrugs, like it's not a big deal, and I wonder if he's embarrassed. I don't ever want him thinking that he has to be ashamed of anything with me. "I think that's pretty special."

He moves back to the topic of Abby. "She didn't even have a name when she showed up, so I just picked Abby. Took me a whole day. I must have read half the internet advice on the topic of naming a baby."

I can't even begin to imagine what I would do if a baby showed up on my doorstep. Would I take her in? Would I call the cops and let them sort it out? "What made you choose Abby? Was that just a gut feeling?"

He smiles down at the little girl, the look instantly softening his harsh features. "I picked Abigail because it means my father's joy. I didn't want her coming into the world with this legacy of being unwanted and abandoned. I wanted to give her something that proved someone is glad she's here."

My heart shatters right there. This man is nothing like I was raised to believe men are. He's good and kind and true and an amazing father.

8
MICAH

"You have seven brothers and sisters?" I repeat as I sit against the headboard of my king-size bed. We're snuggled together under the covers. We're both naked because I had to have her again. She listened when I told her about Abby. She promised to help me find her mother and promised me we'd find a way to legally adopt our little daughter.

My heart about stopped tonight when she called Abby our daughter. It was one of the sweetest moments of my life and no matter how old I get, I'll always treasure it.

"Seven," she confirms with a cute little nod of her head.

I offer her another bite of the fudge covered

brownie. I love watching her lips wrap around the fork. Love imagining that it's my cock instead. One day, we'll have to do that. There's so much I want to explore with this woman. I'm glad I waited. I never quite understood why I wanted to wait but now I do. Some part of my soul knew she was out there.

She makes a soft whimpering noise and when some of the hot fudge dribbles down my chest, she leans forward to lick it off.

I groan at the contact, then her lips go lower, hitting puckered skin. There's sensation, but it's different than on the rest of my body. She hasn't asked about the burns that mar my skin or the obvious grafts I never quite grew into.

She pauses and looks up at me. "Sorry. Does it hurt there?"

"Feels good," I reassure her as I set the dishes on the nightstand. She goes back to pressing kisses, and I thread my fingers through her hair. "Do you want to hear that story?"

She leans back and cups my face, just like I did with her earlier. "Only if you want to share."

It's not a story I've ever told anyone. I never saw the point in it but with Chloe, things are different. I want her to know every part of my life. I want to her to see everything. Because this woman is unflinching in her affection and steadfast in her love. She hasn't said it yet, and I haven't said it either. But I know. I feel it deep in my gut. It's OK though. I can be patient for a little while longer.

"My mom spent most of my childhood high as a kite. So, it fell to me to look after myself and Cassie. One day when I was about nine, I tipped a pot of boiling stew over. Rinsed it off and thought everything was OK until I realized it wasn't."

I was fortunate that a neighbor came in and insisted on taking me to the hospital. But it was the start of a lot of horrible things. Surgeries and grafts and being separated from Cassie.

"Oh, Micah," she whispers.

"That wasn't the worst part. They took us away from her and we went into the system." I shake my head. "Saw so much fucked up shit there. That's why I can't let Abby go into it. Not ever."

"We'll find a way to keep her safe." Her eyes are filled with tears.

I squeeze her hip again as we snuggle deeper into the pillows and blankets. "It doesn't hurt anymore."

"It still shouldn't have happened to you."

"There were good homes," I reassure her. "Some

really great ones. But then there were the ones that were so bad Cassie and I would run away. We'd sleep on the streets. I'll never forget how cold it gets on a park bench."

I think of all the teens I meet who are out there, cold and hungry and alone. Most of them have passed that "cute" age where they're adoptable, and their complex needs from years of trauma means that it takes a very special person to parent them. "When Abby is older, I want to take some of them in. The teenagers."

She puts her head on my shoulder. "We'll do that. We'll adopt as many of them as our house can hold, just like your parents did."

I stroke her hair. "They were a light in the dark. I used to wonder why my life has always been so hard. I thought maybe I was bad and deserved bad things. But more and more, I think it's because I'm meant to help."

She fights a yawn. "You're a good man."

"And you're sleepy."

"Your fault. You wore me out."

"Then sleep. Our daughter will be awake and hungry soon." I press a kiss to her forehead before drifting into a quiet slumber filled with dreams of my little family. If all this suffering was necessary to get to this point, then I'd gladly go through it again. Because I get to be here for little Abby and my beautiful soon-to-be wife. She doesn't know that part yet. But the first chance I get, I'm slipping a ring on this woman's finger. She'll wear my ring and carry my babies and together, we'll build a life.

"Don't you do that," I growl at the mirror. I've just gotten out of the shower and a towel is slung low on my hips. Abby was awake most of the night and finally went to sleep about an hour ago. Her sleep schedule is messed up. But we'll figure out how to fix it. It amazes me how no problem seems insurmountable with Chloe by my side. I'm no longer in this parenting thing alone.

"I'm not doing anything," Chloe protests as she rubs the lotion into her legs. Her long, smooth legs. The ones that were wrapped around my hips just minutes ago. Damn, we're both insatiable. At this rate, I'll have to hire a second manager for the ranch just so I can fuck my woman as often as I want.

I turn and stalk across the room. "You know exactly what you're doing."

"Sorry. I'm being selfish. Do you need some

lotion?" She widens her eyes in innocence before tugging my towel off. My cock springs free, hard and at the ready. Of course, he is. He always will be around Chloe. All it takes is a look from her and I'm in the mood.

She reaches for me, running her slick fingers along my sensitive shaft. "Most people don't know this, but a thorough application is very important when it comes to moisturizing."

"Be as thorough as necessary." My hips buck, almost as if they have a mind of their own. I thrust into her hand, loving the way she can't quite get her fingers fully wrapped around my beast. But damn does she try, teasing and working me until I'm seeing stars and spilling into her hand.

She gives me a triumphant grin. "Next time, it'll be in my mouth."

"Fuck, Chloe. Don't say that." As it is, I'm going to have a permanent hard-on from this woman. If she keeps talking, I'll never be able to wear pants comfortably again.

I reach to return the favor, but her stomach growls. "Breakfast first."

She chuckles and glances from the bathroom to the bedroom. When she's content that Abby isn't making any noises to indicate she's awake, Chloe says, "I think I'll grab a quick shower."

"I'll put on the food," I promise her. She likes toast and orange juice and a hearty helping of oatmeal.

She kisses me, a quick peck on the lips, and I force myself from the room. Otherwise, I'll stay and join her in the shower and then we'll never make it to the kitchen for breakfast.

I'm whistling under my breath as I move around the kitchen. My life these days is perfect. I couldn't ask for anything more.

Then a knock on the door sounds. I frown, wondering if we left one of Abby's things at my parents' place. But when I open the door, it's not either of my parents standing there.

It's a girl. She's young but her face seems familiar. Have I seen her around the ranch before? We're growing so much that I'm no longer on a first-name basis with every employee.

She tucks a strand of red hair behind her ear and manages to get out a single word before she trails off, "I'm..."

I feel Chloe's presence before I even hear her footsteps. Then her hand is pressing into my back as she peers around me. "Do we have a guest for breakfast?"

I frown at the girl. Something about her seems to nag at my memory. "Do we know each other?"

She shifts the strap of her green backpack on her shoulder and avoids my gaze. "I'm the one who left the baby on your porch."

9
CHLOE

I GATHER MY HAIR INTO A LOOSE PONYTAIL, HUMMING a love song under my breath as I peer at my reflection in the bathroom mirror. I don't even look like the same woman who showed up to work here a little over a week ago.

I definitely don't feel like the same woman. Because I'm in love with my boss. With Micah Kringle who is an amazing single dad and a sexy cowboy and an incredible lover. He's everything a girl could possibly want in a man and he's all mine. Together with his daughter, the three of us are going to live happily ever after.

I practically skip into the kitchen, floating on air. But I hear a voice at the front door, so I follow the sound to see Micah standing in front of it. His shoulders are bunched, his entire body filled with tension.

I move behind him, slipping my hand underneath his t-shirt to touch his bare skin. He calms at my touch, his shoulders relaxing slightly. "Do we have a guest for breakfast?"

There's a young woman standing here. She can't be more than a few years younger than me with red hair. Her sneakers are beat up, and her blue jeans have holes in them. Not the fashionable kind though. The kind that come from being worn out. But it's the tired, nervous look in her eyes that has my heart going out to her.

"Do we know each other?" Micah asks.

She fiddles with the strap of her green backpack that's clearly seen better days. Before I can invite her in for breakfast, she says, "I'm the one who left the baby on your porch."

I hear his sharp intake of breath and feel the way Micah freezes beneath my touch. My heart aches, and I send up a silent prayer she hasn't come here to take Abby away from him.

Since neither of them are moving, I say, "Why don't you come in? We can talk about this."

She shakes her head, not looking at either of us. "Is she...happy here?"

Micah says nothing, too frozen to speak or move. I'm not even sure he's breathing right now, and I move my hand in a reassuring circle against his back. I want him to know he's not alone. I'm here with him.

"She's really happy," I offer.

She finally raises her gaze from the porch boards. She looks at me, the tiniest bit of hope flaring in her gaze. "She is?"

"Do you want to see her? She's sleeping but I can get her." I don't know this woman. I'm not entirely sure that Micah does either. But I'm not going to keep a mama from seeing her baby.

"Maybe I could take a quick peek." Her anxious gaze flickers to Micah. "If that's OK."

He crosses his arms over his chest. "When did you leave her on the porch?"

She rattles off the date easily, seeming to shrink in on herself.

"What did you leave her with?"

She answers that question with her shoulders hunched against the biting wind.

I know he's just trying to verify who she is. After all, anyone could appear on his doorstep and claim to be Abby's mother. It's just like Micah to slip into protector mode. But I believe this girl. I think she's exactly who she says she is.

I move my hand from his back and put it on his arm instead.

He looks to me and I give him a little nod, letting him know that I trust her. "Abby will be safe."

"Is that what you named her?" The girl asks.

I hold out my hand, feeling compassion for the girl standing in front of me. I don't know what led her here, why she chose Micah or how she left little Abby behind. But I know she's my daughter's mother. She's given me the most precious gift in all the world, and I'll always be grateful to her for that. "Yes, and I'm Chloe."

She doesn't take my hand, but she does lift her chin. "Sydney."

I give her a smile that I hope is welcoming. "Well, come on in out of the cold and see your daughter. Then we'll have breakfast if you want it."

I still don't know why she's here. But given her hesitation, I don't think she's here for her daughter. At least, I don't believe she's here to take her back. If anything, she's skittish and shy.

Sydney follows me to our bedroom where the crib is. Micah has a spare room that he's been working to turn into a nursery. But he's taking his time and I think it's because he doesn't want her sleeping away from us.

I move to the crib, gesturing for Sydney to come near.

Micah stands in the doorway with his arms crossed again. It's not lost on me that he's blocking the room's exit. He studies her, his face an unreadable mask. This must feel like his worst nightmare.

"You're sure she's happy?" Sydney asks again, peering into the crib.

"She's the sweetest thing," I assure her. "She can lift her head up a little on her own. And she coos at us. I think I even saw her smile the other day. Would you like to hold her?"

She shakes her head. "Babies aren't my thing."

I lead her back into the living room, so we won't disturb Abby and encourage her to take a seat. She perches on the edge of a loveseat, the one nearest the door. She looks like she could bolt at any moment.

I sit across from her on the couch. I gesture for Micah to join me, but he paces the room, agitated and frustrated.

Since he's processing this, I turn to Sydney. "Abby is incredible, and I'm grateful to you. I'm grateful that she's here."

"I'm glad she landed with you two. Guess I did

one thing right for her, huh? I mean, she's cute and all. But I'm not...I wasn't ready."

"That's OK," I reassure her quickly. I don't want her feeling guilt or shame. Not everyone is suited to be a mother, and I don't care how Abby came into my life. I only care that she's a part of it now. "We love her."

Abby lets out a wail, and I glance at Micah. He still looks distraught, so I say, "I'll settle her with a bottle. You talk with Sydney."

Micah

I STARE DOWN AT THE TEENAGE GIRL. FUCK, SHE'S young. Too young for a baby. She looks like she should be graduating high school and packing a beat-up car with furniture for college. Not wandering around homeless and gaunt.

She fiddles with her backpack and a loose string on her pants, anything really. That's when her nervous habits finally jolt my memory.

"Nashville. I was on business for the ranch. Gave you a ride." I don't usually give out rides but something about her made me want to stop. She ran her hand up my thigh as soon as she was in the truck. I made it damn clear we weren't doing anything like that. But I offered her dinner, and we ended up at an all-night diner. We sat for hours, shooting the breeze and talking about nothing important.

She tips her head, studying me. "You do remember me. I didn't expect you to."

Now that I've placed her, everything about that evening comes flooding back. "That was what…eight months ago?"

"Six," she says softly. "I was three and a half months along. I saw you outside of your hotel that night. I thought what if my baby had a dad, someone who cared about her?"

"So, you thought if you came onto me, and we slept together that you could come back later and claim she's mine. Did you think I wouldn't notice?" There's no accusation in my tone, only curiosity.

She hesitates.

"Tell me." I want to hear all of her story. One day, Abby will have questions about her birth mom, and I'll tell her everything. I'll tell her the story of a woman who loved her enough to try and give her a better life.

"I was planning on waiting a year, just long enough for everything to be fuzzy for you. Look, I'm not proud of it, OK? I don't even know her daddy's name. He was just fifty bucks behind the gas station."

I swear under my breath and for a moment, I see it. She's Cassie as a teenager. If I hadn't been there to fend off the men back then, she would have had no one. No protector. No shield. No big brother. My heart aches at the thought. "Where are you staying now?"

The defiant tilt to her chin tells me that was the wrong question. "What's it to you?"

I'm not going to get anywhere with that line of questioning. Shit, she's got to watch her back because she's the only one watching it. At least, she was until she walked into this house. "Why did you pick me? You could have left her anywhere."

"Because you were the first guy in a long time who didn't offer me fifty bucks."

"Well, then you're hanging out with the wrong guys," I tell her and take a seat next to her. She needs a big brother and she just got one. "I'm the manager here. Could use some office help if you're interested in a job."

She wrinkles her nose, little freckles dancing across the bridge of it. Will my Abby have those same freckles one day?

"I don't know a damn thing about offices."

"I didn't either when I started running the place. Suppose you could learn on the job like I did."

She starts digging through her backpack. "Look, I only came back because I realized you can't do anything without her birth certificate. So, I'm here to give you all the paperwork stuff and see if she's happy."

My heart pounds in my chest. She's going to give me everything for Abby, everything that will allow me to legally hold onto her. I'll never have to worry about anyone taking her from me.

"Here's the paperwork the hospital gave me on her. I don't know what to do next to make it legal." She passes it to me then snorts. "And I don't need a big brother."

I accept the crumpled papers and the birth certificate. "Well, you have one now so deal with it."

10
CHLOE

"I can't believe she's really ours," I whisper as I trace her tiny features. She's drinking from her bottle and gazing up at me with peace-filled eyes. Because of Micah, she'll never have to face the indifference of the system or the disappointment of being shuffled from home to home because no one wants her. Well, I guess I'm helping with that since my name went on the adoption papers today.

Sydney and Micah talked in the living room for a few minutes then he came to the bedroom and told me we were going to see a lawyer. The four of us were able to set up what's known as a private adoption. There are still a few requirements to meet within the coming weeks. But we're on the road to legally becoming Abby's parents.

"I might be biased but I think we got the cutest baby ever too," Micah says. We're sitting together on his bed again. The three of us are snuggled under the blankets like a little family. We are a little family, and the thought sends a thrill through me. I never expected that one day Micah and I would be together, let alone raising a beautiful daughter.

Abby grunts as if acknowledging to her father that she is the cutest and she knows it.

Micah croons down at her, "You're going to stay right here with us and you're going to grow up a Kringle. We're going to decorate the nursery in princesses and fairies and anything else you want. Then in the summers, I'll take you fishing, and we'll build a tree fort together. I'll teach you how to throw a ball too. Better than any of the boys."

I laugh at the childhood he's outlined. It sounds wonderful and amazing. It doesn't even surprise me that he's already thinking so far ahead. My Micah loves to plan and scheme. His ability to think into the future is part of what makes this ranch so successful. It'll be a beautiful legacy for my Abby to inherit one day with her cousins. OK, she doesn't have any yet. But with the way West has been looking at Cassie lately, I think it's only a matter of time.

"I think we're finished. You get enough, baby girl?" I ask as she drains the rest of the bottle.

"My turn," Micah calls and takes her in his arms. He keeps her entertained while he burps her and when she's done, he grins at her. "Good job. When you're older, I'll teach you how to burp the alphabet. Uncle Ledger will be jealous of that one."

Her little eyes drift closed, and I don't miss the disappointment that flickers across Micah's face. He loves nothing more than spending time with his little girl. One day soon though she'll be awake all the time and constantly talking to us. I can't wait for those moments.

"Do you think she knows?" He asks softly. "That she was adopted today?"

I don't know how much any baby knows about what's happening. They're doing the important work of growing big and that's tiring. Probably doesn't leave a lot of time to wonder who they belong to. "I think she knows she's loved by the best dad in the world."

He seems satisfied by my answer, gazing at our little girl with such affection on his face. He'd walk through hell for her if she needed him too. No matter how big our daughter grows up to be or how far away she moves, she'll always have his heart, and he'll always have her back.

"Should I call Sydney and see how she's settling in?" I ask as he leaves the bed to put Abby into her crib.

While we were at the lawyer's office, Micah stepped outside to make some phone calls. Next thing I knew his parents were showing up and welcoming Sydney to the family. They didn't ask any questions just accepted it when Micah said this was their granddaughter's biological mother. She'll be staying with them now. She said she'd do it for a few days "on a trial basis". But she also accepted Micah's job offer.

Something tells me that Ledger and West are already spreading the word around the ranch that there's a new Kringle. She'll never be treated with anything less than affection and respect here in Courage County. Who she was before doesn't matter. She's been given a new name. The Kringle name.

"I'll check in on her tomorrow morning," he answers as he settles Abby in her crib.

"Then I guess we have to figure out what we're going to do with a long, lonely night stretched out in front of us," I tell him, barely able to keep the smirk off my face.

He straightens and turns to me, the soft lamp light making him look boyish and much younger than his nearly thirty years. "Oh, I can think of some bedtime activities, Mrs. Kringle."

It takes me a minute to understand what he's saying. I think he just called me his future wife. "That...You didn't ask me."

He stalks toward the bed. "Why would I ask you? You're already mine. We'll just be making it official."

"That's not much of a proposal," I argue just to be contrary. I'm already looking forward to spending decades with Micah, arguing with him every day and falling more in love.

"Perhaps I need to find other ways to convince you then," he says as he crawls onto the bed. He drapes his big body over mine. His hardness settles between my thighs and there's an answering rush of wet heat in my panties.

"I might be open to other forms of persuasion," I agree as I spread my legs wider.

"Good, then let's begin negotiations." He kisses his way down my throat and reaches for the tie on my robe. He opens it, letting out a delighted moan when he realizes I'm not wearing anything underneath it. If Abby hadn't needed a bottle, something tells me he would have figured that one out earlier.

"What—what terms are you proposing?" It's hard to think with his lips on my neck, driving me crazy like this.

"First term, daily orgasms for you." He kisses and licks and nips his way down the valley of my chest. He pauses to give my nipples his attention, teasing me there too. He finally grazes his teeth over one hardened point. "How do you feel about that term, Mrs. Kringle?"

I gasp at the sensation and struggle to remember what we were talking about. Oh, yeah, the negotiations. "I'm in favor of that term, Mr. Kringle."

He releases my breast with a wet popping sound. "Excellent, and the next term is this..." He prowls lower, pressing kisses to my curvy stomach. He worships every stretchmark and every bit of cellulite with his tongue until he's at the juncture of my thighs.

"Next term is I get to eat this pussy daily for the rest of my life." Then he licks a stripe across my swollen mound, and I arch my back, shoving my pussy into his face.

He doesn't mind though. He just wraps his big hands around my hips and anchors me to the bed then he falls on me like a wild animal. He snarls and growls with every lick, letting me know exactly how much he's enjoying his meal. It's not until I'm thrashing against the pillows, begging him for mercy that he finally sucks my engorged clit into his mouth.

I come so hard he has to throw a hand over my mouth to keep me quiet. Somehow that only sends me higher, prolonging the orgasm.

When I float down, he's aligning his body to mine and slipping inside of my aching channel.

"And the final unalterable term is that this pussy belongs to me. Only. Me." He punctuates the words with a quick thrust of his hips.

"Only you," I agree as the next wave of pleasure begins to build inside of me. This man is incredible. The way he can control my body so easily, pushing me higher and higher.

"Need you to come for me," he grunts. Sweat has soaked his hair, leaving it damp across his forehead. His beard is glistening from my juices, but it's the reverence in his eyes that steals my breath away. This man doesn't just love me. He cherishes me. I don't just know that. I feel it, deep in my soul. In that place where our two hearts have intertwined and become one.

"I love you," I whisper just as I come on his cock like he wanted.

He swells inside of me then, his hot seed spilling into my body. He's murmuring things under his breath as he bucks wildly. I think he's making promises to love me and protect me and care for me. All of his words blend together, a beautiful confession.

When he finally collapses onto the sheets next to me, he pulls me against him. The overhead fan cools our sweat-slicked bodies as I listen to his heartbeat.

"Love you, too." He presses a kiss to my forehead.

I smile so big that my cheeks hurt. "Then I accept your proposal, Mr. Kringle."

"And all the terms?" He teases.

"And all the terms," I agree as I drift to sleep with a smile on my face and one in my heart. This gruff cowboy and his daughter are my family, and I can't wait to spend the rest of our lives together.

EPILOGUE

CHLOE

"There you are. Missed you this morning." Micah presses a soft kiss to my shoulder as he wraps his arms around me from behind. He's shirtless today, and I can feel his body heat through my thin sweater.

"I missed you too," I whisper back even though my mom is nearby at the stove. She's making pancakes for me and my siblings. It's Christmas Eve, and my whole family is here.

"Tonight, I get you," he says in a low tone before he kisses me on the lips. I bunked in the living room last night with my mom. When she first arrived, she was worried about me. But now that she's met Micah and seen how good he is to me, she seems genuinely happy for me.

"Gross!" One of my brothers yells from his spot at the kitchen table.

There's a whizzing sound then Micah's hand is up, catching the foam ball before it can make contact with me. "Boys, don't throw things at your sister."

"Why not?" My nine-year-old brother Benji taunts.

Micah turns around and glares at the table. He's all bark when it comes to my siblings. Even though they've been staying with us all week, he hasn't complained once. No, he's embraced all of them like they're his own family. "Because you'll give someone a black eye on my wedding day, and that will make me cranky."

"Not to mention, Santa will skip the house tonight," Mama adds as she slides another perfectly golden pancake onto the platter and passes it to Micah. "Eat up. We got a big day."

He asked her to move here. He offered to build her a house on the Kringle Ranch and pay her relocation costs. Mama said no but I could tell she was tempted. He told her the offer will always stand.

Things are different now with my family. An anonymous benefactor went through and paid off the family home and caught my mama up on her overdue bills. Then they helped her enroll in night courses so she can get a higher paying job in a few years. The person even set up a scholarship system so each of my siblings can go to college if they want.

Both Mama and I know that it was Micah, but every time I try to bring it up, he acts like he doesn't know what I'm talking about. He won't ever admit it because he doesn't want me to feel indebted to him.

He settles at the kitchen table across from Benji. Then he immediately pulls me into his lap and feeds me from his plate. My family doesn't even comment on it. They go on like this is normal because in the past week, they've gotten used to seeing Micah do this. He loves taking care of me and dotes on me all the time.

"I got a question, Micah," Benji says. "How much would you pay me to not wear my clown mask today?"

"Oh, you can wear it," Micah answers. "You just can't wear it anytime during the ceremony or photos."

Benji scowls at him, and I laugh before I kiss Micah again. I can taste the syrup on his lips. He squeezes my thigh under the table but neither of us try to go any further. Still, my heart is pounding when I pull away from him. "I'll go wake our little princess, so she doesn't miss the ceremony."

"So, what do you think?" I ask as I twirl around in my wedding dress with the full skirt and sweetheart neckline. Creating a wedding in just a few weeks should have been hard but it wasn't. It helps that Cassie and West also got married today. In fact, everyone just celebrated their vows. Now I'm in the back and it's my turn.

"Fits you like a glove," Cassie says.

"You look incredible," Peyton gushes.

"Love the shoes." Sydney nods to my sequined heels. She's the one who found them for me. She's a regular part of my life now. She works with Micah at the office and lives with his parents. She sees Abby frequently and she's happy that we're adopting her.

We've made every effort to locate Abby's birth father and give him a chance to come forward. So far though, we haven't had any luck and at this point, I doubt we will. But Abby still seems like a happy baby, and I know Micah loves her just as fiercely as if she were his flesh and blood.

Abby squeals her agreement. She's getting old enough to be a part of more events. I love watching her discover more of the world and getting to be the one who introduces it to her. Yesterday, I read her a story book about Santa. I'm not sure she understood what I was saying but she did stare in fascination at the big, jolly man.

Mama chuckles and passes my little drool machine to Peyton to hold.

The girls exchange a look before excusing themselves.

Mama reaches into her purse and produces her gold necklace, the one with the ruby teardrop pendant. She's worn it for years and before that, my grandmother. "It's yours now."

I admire the sparkling jewelry for a moment before I turn my back to her and shift my hair so she can put it around my neck.

"I didn't want to like him," she admits as she fastens the clasp.

"I know." She didn't exactly hide her dislike or distrust of Micah, even after she suspected he was the one who paid off all the bills and made life easier for my family. Southern pride runs deep, even deeper when poverty is involved.

Still, it's nice to see her without those worry lines on her face. Nice to see her laughing easily and not worrying about every dime she's spending when she's shopping with me. She's finally getting to enjoy life a little bit, and I love that for her.

"But it's hard to hate the man who loves your daughter so fiercely. I think he'd give you the world if you demanded it, lay siege to cities with only a word from you."

I turn to her as my eyes fill with tears. I have to blink to keep them from falling. "He's my whole world."

She reaches out to pat my cheek. "That's good. Because you're his."

There's a knock on the door then Mrs. Kringle is poking her head in and telling us we can start any time I'm ready. I glance at my mom, my heart so full of love it feels like I'll float away. "I'm definitely ready."

When the doors of the chapel finally swing open and I can see Micah, my first instinct is to run to him. That will always be my instinct when I see him.

He gives me a smile that's blinding, lighting up the tiny auditorium.

I can't help smiling back as I pledge to love and cherish this man. He promises the same to me, and the intensity in his gaze as he says those two words nearly brings me to my knees. He means them. For now and forever.

After the ceremony, he takes my hand and whispers in my ear, "I love you, Mrs. Kringle. You've always been mine. It's just official now."

I tug him toward the bridal suite while everyone is distracted. "Sneak away with me for a minute. We have more terms to negotiate, Mr. Kringle."

His chuckle warms me all over. "I'd never argue with my bride."

I can't help grinning as I close the door behind us. He's mine now, and I'm his, and our life together will always be an adventure. But our first adventure is starting right now in the bridal suite.

Want a bonus scene with Micah and Chloe? Sign up for my weekly newsletter and get the bonus here.

READ NEXT: A CHRISTMAS BABY FOR THE COWBOY

Geeky bartender seeks virile cowboy. Must love gingerbread, ugly sweaters, and making out by the fire.

Peyton

My best friend and I have a pact. Every year, he gets me something I really want for Christmas and well, this year I'd like to have a baby. Except I don't want it to be just anybody's baby. I want it to be Ledger's baby.

I'm not bold enough to tell him this until I get a little bit drunk one night and spill the beans. I thought he'd turn me down but the next morning, I wake to discover that Ledger is considering it.

He has conditions but only one of them makes me gulp: Ledger wants to make our child the old-fashioned way with lots of long, sweaty moments. But will the chemistry that burns between us forever change our friendship?

Ledger

My best friend wants me to breed her. A noble man would tell her no. Good thing no one has ever accused me of being that.

I know this moment with Peyton is exactly what I've been waiting for, so I insist on conditions. Mainly that we try making the baby the old-fashioned way. After all, this is my chance to finally convince my best friend that we're meant to be.

If you're looking for a dual virgin romance novella with a cinnamon roll hero, it's time to meet Ledger in A Christmas Baby for the Cowboy.

Read Peyton and Ledger's Story

COURAGE COUNTY SERIES

Welcome to Courage County where protective alpha heroes fall for strong curvy women they love and defend. There's NO cheating and NO cliffhangers. Just a sweet, sexy HEA in each book.

Love on the Ranch

Her Alpha Cowboy

Pregnant and alone, Riley has nowhere to go until the alpha cowboy finds her. Will she fall in love with her rescuer?

Her Older Cowboy

Summer is making a baby with her brother's best friend. But he insists on making it the old-fashioned way.

Her Protector Cowboy

Jack will do whatever it takes to protect his curvy woman after their hot one-night stand…then he plans to claim her!

Her Forever Cowboy

Dean is in love with his best friend's widow. When they're stranded together for the night, will he finally tell her how he feels?

Her Dirty Cowboy

The ranch's newest hire also happens to be the woman Adam had a one-night stand with…and she's carrying his baby!

Her Sexy Cowboy

She's a scared runaway with a baby. He's determined to protect them both. But neither of them expected to fall in love.

Her Wild Cowboy

He'll keep his curvy woman safe, even if it means a marriage in name only. But what happens when he wants to make it a real marriage?

Her Wicked Cowboy

One hot night with Jake gave me the best gift of my life: a beautiful baby girl. Will he want us to be a family when I show up on his doorstep a year later?

Courage County Brides

The Cowboy's Bride

The only way out of my horrible life is to become a mail order bride. But will my new cowboy husband be willing to take a chance on love?

The Cowboy's Soulmate

Can a jaded playboy find forever with his curvy mail order bride and her baby? Or will her secret ruin their future?

The Cowboy's Valentine

I'm a grumpy loner cowboy and I like it that way. Until my beautiful mail order bride arrives and suddenly, I want more than a marriage in name only.

The Cowboy's Match

Will this mail order bride matchmaker take a chance on love when she falls for the bearded cowboy who happens to be her VIP client?

The Cowboy's Obsession

Can this stalker cowboy show the curvy schoolteacher that he's the one for her?

The Cowboy's Sweetheart

Rule #1 of becoming a mail order bride: never fall in love with your cowboy groom.

The Cowboy's Angel

Can this cowboy single dad with a baby find love with his new mail order bride?

The Cowboy's Heiress

This innocent heiress is posing as a mail order bride. But what happens when her grumpy cowboy husband discovers who she really is?

Courage County Warriors

Rescue Me

Getting out was hard. Knowing who to trust was easy: my dad's best friend. He's the only man I can count on, but will we be able to keep our hands off each other?

Protect Me

When I need a warrior to protect me, I know just who to turn to: my brother's best friend. But will this grumpy cowboy who's guarding my body break my heart?

Shield Me

When trouble comes for me, I know who to call—my ex-boyfriend's dad. He's the only one who can help. But can I convince this grumpy cowboy to finally claim me?

Courage County Fire & Rescue

The Firefighter's Curvy Nanny

As a single dad firefighter, I was only looking for a quick fling. Then the curvy woman from last night shows up. Turns out, she's my new nanny.

The Firefighter's Secret Baby

After a scorching one-night stand with a sexy firefighter, I realize I'm pregnant…with my brother's best friend's baby.

The Firefighter's Forbidden Fling

I knew a one night stand with my grumpy boss wasn't the best idea…but I didn't think it would lead to anything serious. I definitely didn't think it would lead to a surprise pregnancy with this sexy firefighter.

GET A FREE COWBOY ROMANCE

Get Her Grumpy Cowboy for FREE:
https://www.MiaBrody.com/free-cowboy/

LIKE THIS STORY?

If you enjoyed this story, please post a review about it. Share what you liked or didn't like. It may not seem like much, but reviews are so important for indie authors like me who don't have the backing of a big publishing house.

Of course, you can also share your thoughts with me via email if you'd prefer to reach out that way. My email address is mia @ miabrody.com (remove the spaces). I love hearing from my readers!

ABOUT THE AUTHOR

Mia Brody writes steamy stories about alpha men who fall in love with big, beautiful women. She loves happy endings and every couple she writes will get one!

When she's not writing, Mia is searching for the perfect slice of cheesecake and reading books by her favorite instalove authors.

Keep in touch when you sign up for her newsletter: https://www.MiaBrody.com/news. It's the fastest way to hear about her new releases so you never miss one!

Made in United States
Troutdale, OR
12/08/2023